To my high school Spanish teachers, Mrs. Schirmer, Mrs. Houlihan, and Mrs. Wereszynski:
Tus nombres estarán en las escuelas y bibliotecas para siempre. —J. F.

A Feiwel and Friends Book
An imprint of Macmillan Publishing Group, LLC
120 Broadway, New York, NY 10271 • mackids.com

Our books may be purchased in bulk for promotional, educational, or business use.
Please contact your local bookseller or the Macmillan Corporate and Premium Sales Department
at (800) 221-7945 ext. 5442 or by email at MacmillanSpecialMarkets@macmillan.com.

Library of Congress Cataloging-in-Publication Data is available.

First edition, 2022
Book design by Rich Deas
The illustrations for this book were created digitally
Feiwel and Friends logo designed by Filomena Tuosto
Printed in China by RR Donnelley Asia Printing Solutions Ltd., Dongguan City, Guangdong Province

ISBN 978-1-250-83041-8 (hardcover)

1 3 5 7 9 10 8 6 4 2

CON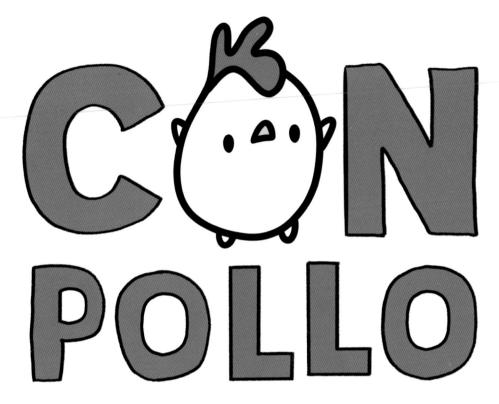 POLLO

A Bilingual Playtime Adventure

JIMMY FALLON
and
JENNIFER LOPEZ

Illustrated by Andrea Campos

FEIWEL AND FRIENDS
NEW YORK

This is Pollo. She wants to play.

And play

and play

and play all day!

Pollo is friendly. Pollo is fun.

Want an example? I'll give you one.

Isn't this fun? Let's help with the words.

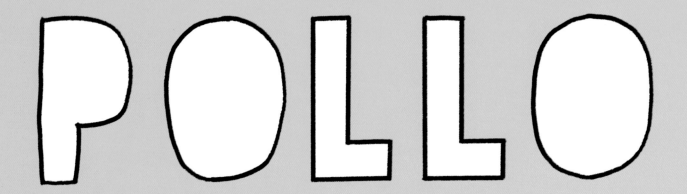

POLLO

rhymes with

FRO♥YO.

It's a chicken. A bird.

Con means "with" and
sounds a little like "cone."
There's so many things to do
that you don't have to alone.

Do you want to play soccer?

Play fútbol con Pollo?

Do you want to go skateboarding?

Patinar con Pollo?

Do you want to go dancing?

Bailar con Pollo?

It's a busy day for you and this chicken.

You want to play more?
Hurry! Time is a-tickin'!

Do you want to go to school?

OR

Go to la escuela con Pollo?

Do you want to go to the library?

Go to la biblioteca con Pollo?

Do you want to go to the store?

TOY STORE

Go to la tienda con Pollo?

You seemed to have fun
playing with all the

TOYS, SO...

let's see what else you can do

CON
POLLO.

Do you want to build something?

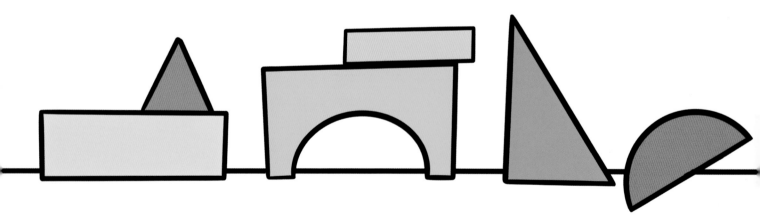

Construir con Pollo?

Do you want to fly?

OR

Volar con Pollo?

Do you want to look at the stars?

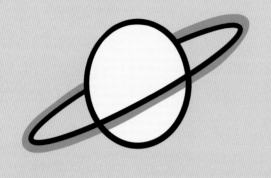

Look at las estrellas con Pollo?

Pollo is soooooo tired!
It's time to lie down and sleep.

Do you hear a noise?
I hear a "Cheep! Cheep!"

Let's say good night.
Tomorrow's another day.

You can read this again—this time

will play!

THE
END

¡pío pío!

TRANSLATIONS

 beach – la playa
(lah PLAH-yah)

soccer – el fútbol
(el FOOT-bohl)

 skateboarding – patinar
(pah-tee-NAHR)

dancing – bailar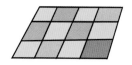
(bye-LAHR)

 school – la escuela
(lah ehs-KWEH-lah)

library – la biblioteca
(lah BEE-blee-oh-TEH-kah)

store – la tienda
(lah tee-YEN-dah)

 build – construir
(Kohn-stroo-EER)

fly – volar
(boh-LAHR)

 stars – las estrellas
(las ehs-TREH-yahs)

chick – el pollito
(el poh-YEE-toh)

 the end – fin
(feen)

cheep cheep – pío pío
(PEE-oh PEE-oh)